Library of Congress Cataloging-in-Publication Data
Pirotta, Saviour.   Little bird/by Saviour Pirotta;
illustrated by Stephen Butler.—1st U.S. ed.
p. cm.   SUMMARY: Several animals describe their favorite
activities to a little bird that asks, "What can I do today?"
ISBN 0-688-11289-7 (trade)—0-688-11290-0 (lib.)
[1. Birds—Fiction.   2. Animals—Fiction.]
I. Butler, Stephen, 1962-   ill. II. Title.
PZ7.P6425Li 1992 [E]—dc20
91-25413 CIP AC
First U.S. edition, 1992
1 3 5 7 9 10 8 6 4 2

Little Bird

by Saviour Pirotta
illustrated by Stephen Butler

Tambourine Books  New York

"What can I do today?" asked the little bird.

"Hop," said the bug.

"Wriggle," said the worm.

"Jump," said the frog.

"Bristle," said the hedgehog.

"Paddle," said the duck.

"Skip," said the lamb.

"Roll," said the pig.

"Gallop," said the horse.

"Munch," said the cow.

"Fly," said the little bird's mother. "Fly."

So the little bird flew around the farm
and across the fields.

And back home
just in time for bed.